D

E

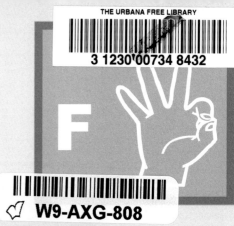

F

I

N

O

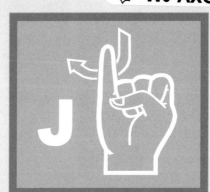

P

S

X

Y

Z

Sophie

Through Sophie's Eyes

D A N C E

Teaching dance to the preschoolers at The School For the Deaf has inspired me to write this story.

Author Catherine Gibson
Illustrations by Robert Noreika

Published by For Children With Love Publications

P.O Box 1552 | Farmington,Ct 06032

www.forchildrenwithlove.com

Composed in the United States
Printed in the United States

FIRST IMPRESSION 2009

ISBN 13: 978-0-578-00980-3

Through Sophie's Eyes

Author Catherine Gibson
Illustrations by Robert Noreika

A special thank you to my family for their love and encouragement throughout the process of writing and publishing this book, I love you!! 🤟 Thank you Wendy Ku, and Cassy Baptista for all of your help and enthusiasm while working with me. Thank you Robert Noreika for your artwork and for bringing the story to life with your wonderful artistic talents. To Erin Bell Photography for your beautiful work. Thank you to Scott Sierakowski for your creative work with the book layout and website. To my author friends, Elizabeth Faragher, Sandy Maineri and Tom Jacobson, thank you for your guidance and support. To my nieces, Alyssa and Kylee, thank you for modeling, I love you!!! 🤟 To "Miss Helyn" Flanagan, who taught my sister Terri and I dance all throughout our lives, you are inspirational!!! To this day, Helyn Flanagan is still teaching dance with my mother Joan Czerwinski and bringing happiness to peoples lives. Thank you to the American School For the Deaf in West Hartford, Connecticut, for allowing me to teach dance to the "Teddy Bear" preschool group. It brought joy that will always be treasured within my heart.

We started a foundation called "For Children With Love," which proceeds from each book will be donated to various causes for children. For more information, contact us at www.forchildrenwithlove.com.

In a small town, not too far from here, lived a girl named Sophie. She was like most other girls her age except she could not hear or speak. Sophie was deaf. To communicate, she would read people's lips and speak with her hands using sign language.

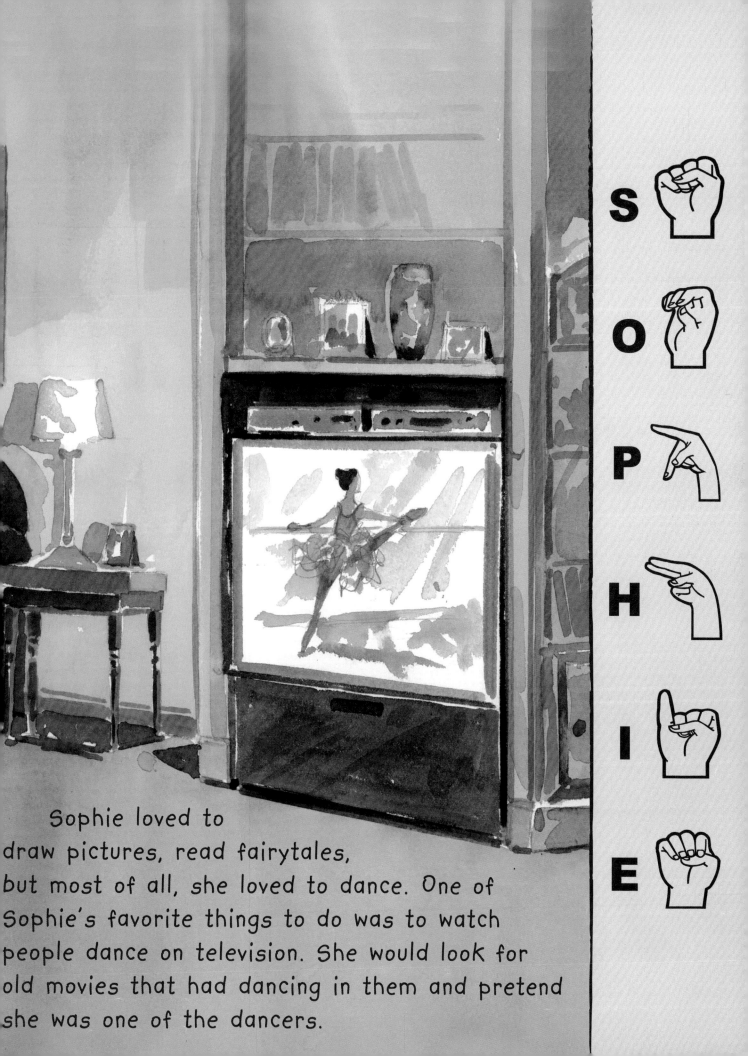

S
O
P
H
I
E

Sophie loved to draw pictures, read fairytales, but most of all, she loved to dance. One of Sophie's favorite things to do was to watch people dance on television. She would look for old movies that had dancing in them and pretend she was one of the dancers.

Once Sophie went to a
beautiful wedding and was fascinated by all the people
spinning and twirling on the dance floor. She watched as the
ladies were spun around in their pretty dresses and high-heeled
shoes. She was in awe with their gentle and graceful manner.

D A N C E

While everyone was dancing, Sophie found herself
feeling the vibrations of the music coming
through the dance floor. She, too, was swaying
and dancing just like the other guests.

Sophie's mom also loved to dance. The two of them would dance together for hours. They would move the furniture around and turn the living room into a dance area. One day Sophie's mom decided to surprise Sophie with a little dance area in her bedroom.

While Sophie was at school, her mom had long mirrors and a wooden ballet barre put in her room. It looked like a real dance studio.

When Sophie came home that day, she was so surprised. She never could have imagined having her own dance studio. The only thing that was missing were other dancers to dance with.

The next day Sophie went to school with a big smile on her face. She still couldn't believe she had her very own dance area.

As she sat at her desk, the teacher passed out a flyer to the class. The flyer was from the local dance studio. They were offering dance lessons to the students at her school. Sophie was so excited. She couldn't wait to share the news with her mom!

Science
Read Pgs.
21-34

Quiz!!
Friday

S
C
H
O
O
L

While on the bus traveling home, Sophie started daydreaming about taking dance lessons at the dance studio. When the bus stopped in front of Sophie's house, she leaped off the bus and went running inside. She ran right to her mom and handed her the flyer. Sophie quickly signed, "Can I take dance lessons? Can I?"

At first her mom was worried and signed, "The girls that take dance lessons can hear the music. They can listen for the teacher's instructions. It might be too hard for you."

Sophie signed back, "Mom, I could watch the teacher and follow. I don't need to hear the music, I can feel it."

Her mom smiled and signed back, "Okay, we can try it."

Sophie jumped up and down and signed to her mom, "Thank you! Thank you!"

The next day after school, Sophie's mom took her to the dance studio. As Sophie entered, she stopped and looked all around the room. The dance room was just as she imagined. It was a large room with floor to ceiling mirrors and a wooden ballet barre that went down the entire side of the wall. The dance teacher went over to greet them.

N
A
M
E

Sophie signed, "Hello, My name is Sophie. I am excited to take dance lessons."

The teacher signed back, "Hello Sophie. My name is Miss Helyn. I am glad you are excited to take dance lessons. We will have lots of fun." Sophie and her mom were happily surprised that Miss Helyn knew sign language.

It was time for the dance lesson to begin. Miss Helyn brought Sophie to the center of the room and introduced her to the class.

Sophie signed to the girls, "Hello, my name is Sophie." The girls looked puzzled as Sophie used sign language to greet them. When the class started, Miss Helyn signed to Sophie to line up with the other girls at the ballet barre.

While the girls were in line, they whispered to one another, covering their mouths so Sophie couldn't read their lips. Sophie knew they were whispering about her. She tried to be brave, but tears began to slowly roll down her cheeks.

Miss Helyn noticed Sophie was upset. She signed to Sophie, "Are you okay? Do you want to stop for the day?"

Sophie dried her tears and signed back to Miss Helyn, "I will be okay. I want to dance."

Miss Helyn noticed the girls were not being that nice to Sophie. When class ended for the day, Sophie quickly grabbed her stuff and left. Miss Helyn asked the other girls to stay. She told the girls to start stretching and she would be right back.

She went to her office and returned shortly with a bag of cotton. She had all the girls take a piece of cotton and put it in their ears. Miss Helyn told the girls they would be dancing without music, like Sophie.

T
E
A
C
H
E
R

Miss Helyn signaled the girls to line up in the center of the room. She told them they could not rely on their ears to listen for the music or instruction. They had to use their other senses and feel the rhythm of the movements. Miss Helyn used her hand movements and body language to guide the girls.

The girls began to stumble over one another as they tried to keep their eyes focused on Miss Helyn. They were tired and out of breath as they tried to find the rhythm. They did not realize how difficult it was to dance without hearing the music.

L E A R N

When Sophie got home, her mom asked, "How was dance class?" Sophie told her mom how the girls treated her and she began to cry.

She signed to her mom, "The girls think because I'm deaf, I can't dance!"

Her mom replied as she softly wiped away the tears from her face, "Oh Sophie, you are a wonderful dancer. Don't worry about what the other girls think. Not being able to hear is only a part of who you are. You have a special gift that allows you to use dancing as a way to express yourself. You should celebrate who you are, I do."

D
E
A
F

The next day, Sophie decided to walk to dance class. She knew she could show the girls that she was a good dancer. As she was walking, it started to rain.

R A I N

The rain was like music to Sophie. She looked up and smiled as the rain drops tip-toed on her face. Sophie leaped and splashed through the puddles all the way to dance class.

When Sophie arrived at the dance studio, she quickly changed from her wet shoes to her ballet slippers. While stretching for class, Sophie noticed that the other girls were smiling at her. One of them even waved and motioned for her to stand next to her at the wooden barre.

Miss Helyn began the class, and everyone watched for her instructions. Sophie noticed that Miss Helyn did not turn the music on. She also noticed that Miss Helyn did not give any verbal instructions. She was only using her body movements and hand signals. It put a smile on Sophie's face when she realized that the girls were learning to dance through her eyes. They were seeing what it was like for her everyday.

As the weeks went by, the girls prepared for their solo performances. Sophie practiced and practiced. It was finally Sophie's day to do her solo performance. She thought to herself, "I can do this. I love to dance! I am ready." Sophie was nervous yet excited.

She slowly walked to the center of the room and saw everyone's eyes on her. She got into her dance position, took a deep breath, and waited to feel the music. And then she danced, and danced, and danced! The girls watched in awe. They started whispering again, but this time they did not cover their mouths. They were all saying that Sophie was beautiful! She was graceful! She was a ballerina!

At the end of Sophie's dance, she glanced over to the other dancers to see their reaction. She saw smiles on their faces, as they clapped and cheered for her. Sophie could not have been happier! As she curtsied, the dancers ran to the center of the room to join her. They all formed a circle holding each other's hands and danced together. Everyone realized that you do not need to be able to hear the music to be a great dancer. The girls curtsied goodbye to Miss Helyn, hugged each other, and left class with a great lesson learned.

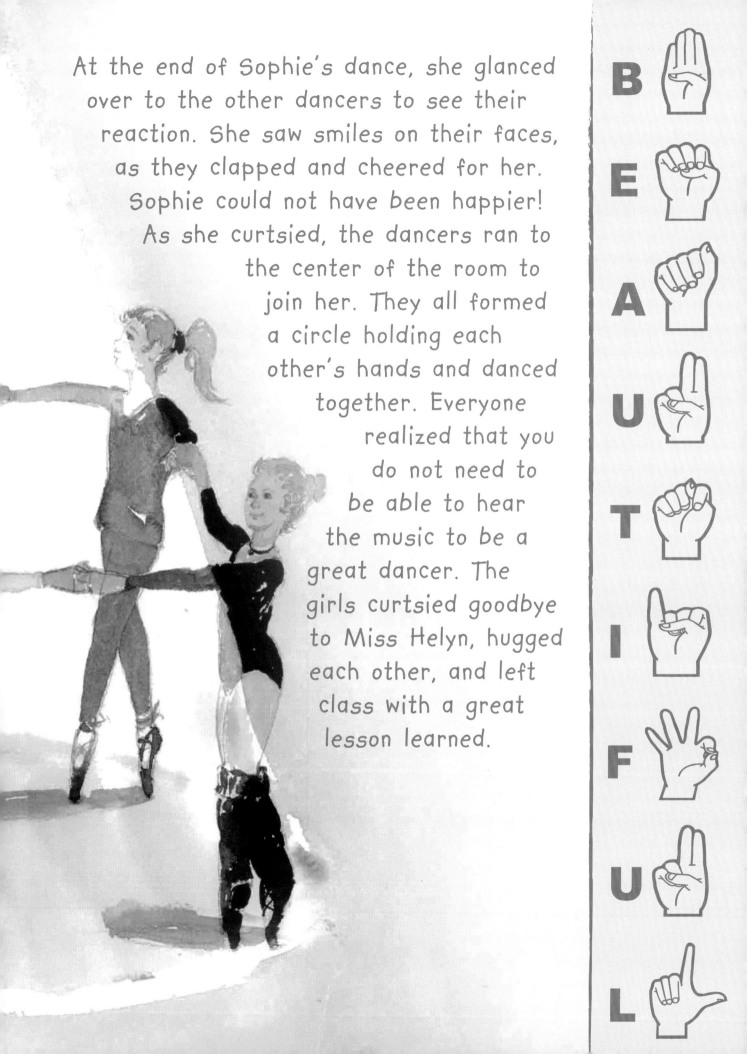

B
E
A
U
T
I
F
U
L

That night as Sophie's mom tucked her into bed, Sophie told her mom how proud she felt about her performance and how she loved her dance class. "The girls were so happy for me!" Sophie signed.

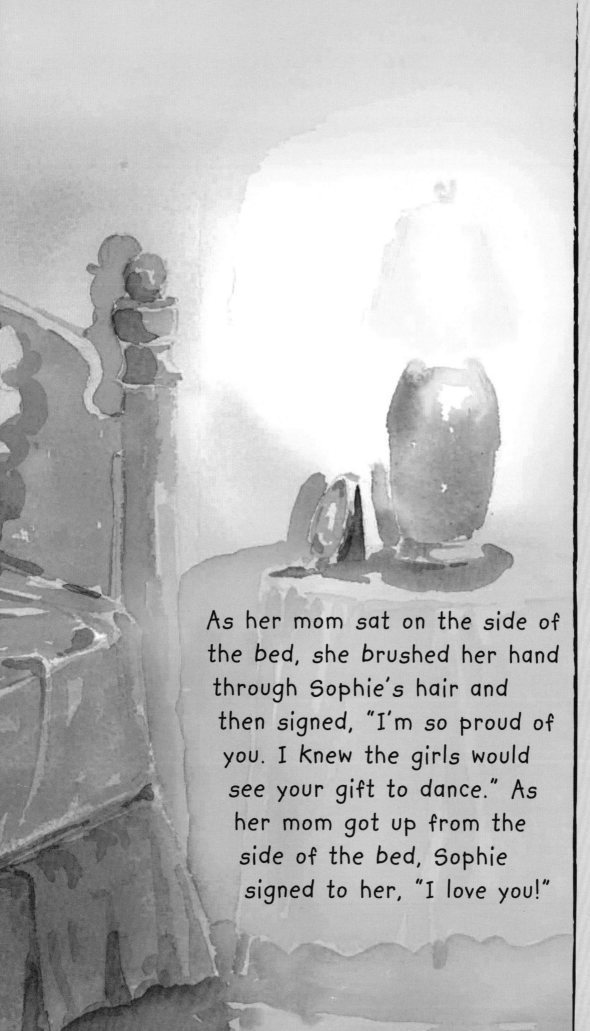

As her mom sat on the side of the bed, she brushed her hand through Sophie's hair and then signed, "I'm so proud of you. I knew the girls would see your gift to dance." As her mom got up from the side of the bed, Sophie signed to her, "I love you!"

I LOVE YOU

Author Bio

Catherine Gibson took dance lessons since the age of
three. She has also taught dance to preschool children for
many years. The characters in this story are based
on people who have touched and inspired her. Cathy has
always been fascinated with sign language. When her children
became older, she decided to take sign language courses at The
American School For The Deaf in West Hartford, Connecticut.
While taking courses, she was introduced to the preschool
program and decided to teach dance to the children through
signing and body movement. After teaching at the school, Cathy
wanted to spread the word that deaf children loved to dance .
The children in her class, gave her the inspiration to write this story.

Illustrator Bio

Robert Noreika is a watercolorist who attended the Paier
College of Art in Hamden, Connecticut. He has an art studio
in the Arts Center in Avon, Connecticut. He lives with his
wife Chris and his fourteen year-old daughter, Sarah. This is
his eleventh book he has illustrated.

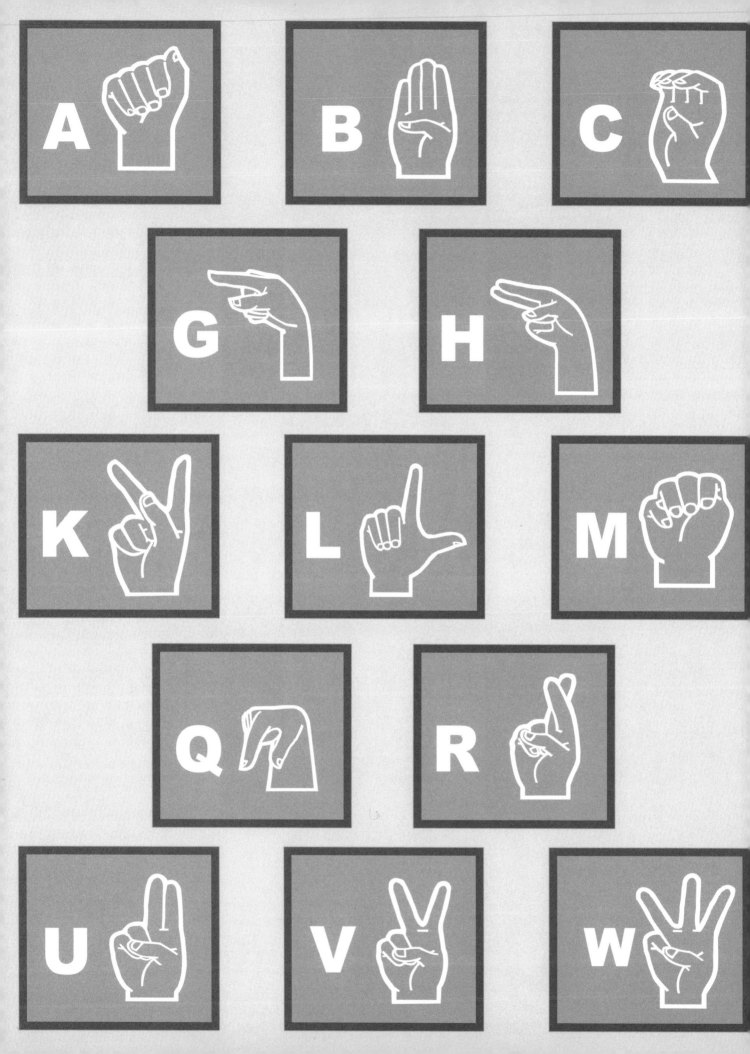